Richard Scarry's
Dr. Doctor

A Golden Book • New York

Western Publishing Company, Inc., Racine, Wisconsin 53404

Western Publishing offers a wide range of fine juvenile and adult activities, games, and puzzles. For more information write Golden Press, 120 Brighton Road, Dept. M, Clifton, NJ 07012.

Freddie Fox
Visits Dr. Doctor

Freddie Fox is in the doctor's office.
His mother is with him.
They are waiting for the doctor.

Other people are waiting, too.
The doctor is late.

The telephone rings.
Dr. Doctor's nurse answers it.
She says, "Which Dr. Doctor
do you want to see?

Mr. Dr. Doctor helps mothers
when they have babies.
Mrs. Dr. Doctor helps children
stay well."

The doctor is coming.
No. Two doctors are coming!

"Good morning," says Mr. Dr. Doctor.
"Good morning," says Mrs. Dr. Doctor.
"Good morning," say all the people
who are waiting.

Freddie and his mother get up.
They follow Mrs. Dr. Doctor.

"How do you feel, Freddie?"
asks Mrs. Dr. Doctor.
"I feel fine," says Freddie.
"Well, let me see," says the doctor.

"Open wide!" the doctor tells Freddie.
She looks in his mouth.
She looks in his ears.
She looks all over him.

"Freddie, you look just fine!"
says the doctor.
"My, you are also getting
big and strong.
Now, do not get sick.
Then I will not have
to see you for a while.

"Now I have a surprise for
both of you.
I am going to have a baby,"
the doctor says.

"Oh, boy!" says Freddie.
"Will it be a girl or a boy?"
"We do not care," says Mrs. Dr. Doctor.
"Just as long as it is well, like you."

"Will Mr. Dr. Doctor help
when you have the baby?" asks Freddie.
"He will be there if he can,"
says Mrs. Dr. Doctor.
"But only just like any other father.

"Our friend Dr. Bandage will help,"
says Mrs. Dr. Doctor.
"He is a good doctor.
He helps a lot of mothers
when they have babies."

"May I play with the baby?"
asks Freddie.
"When the baby gets old enough,"
says Mrs. Dr. Doctor.
"Then he, or she, may
play with you."

Isn't that nice?

A Hospital Story

One day Mr. Dr. Doctor
was at the hospital.
He had just helped Mrs. Bunny.
Mrs. Bunny had five new babies.

Then Mr. Dr. Doctor got a call.
It was Mrs. Dr. Doctor.
"Our baby is coming," she said.
"Stay at the hospital.
My sister Sally will take me there."

Mr. Dr. Doctor was very happy.
Then he got another call.
"My mother needs you,"
said a little girl.
Her name was Molly.
Now, Mr. Dr. Doctor wanted
to be with Mrs. Dr. Doctor.
But he had to help Molly's mother first.

So Mr. Dr. Doctor got into an ambulance.
He was on his way to Molly's house.

Meanwhile, Mrs. Dr. Doctor
got into Sally's car.
They were on their way
to the hospital.

Mr. Dr. Doctor saw Sally's car.
He called to Mrs. Dr. Doctor,
"I hope it is a boy."
But Mrs. Dr. Doctor was hoping
for a girl.

Mr. Dr. Doctor got to Molly's house.
He ran in the front door.
He tripped.
"Where is your mother?" he asked.
"In the bedroom," said Molly.

Mr. Dr. Doctor was just in time.
Molly's mother had a baby.

Mr. Dr. Doctor took everyone
to the hospital.
They would rest there.

Mr. Dr. Doctor went to
Mrs. Dr. Doctor's room.
He tripped.
Dr. Bandage was there.

Look! Mrs. Dr. Doctor has a new baby.
No! She has *two* new babies—
a boy *and* a girl!
Mr. and Mrs. Dr. Doctor are very happy.

It is a few months later.
Mr. and Mrs. Dr. Doctor come to work.
They have their babies,
Billy and Bonnie, with them.
I think Billy and Bonnie will grow up
to be good doctors, just like their
mommy and daddy.
Don't you hope so?